Freddi the Dog

Eats Everything

(and I mean everything!!!)

Fredericka Books

Published by Fredericka Books

Text copyright 2009 by Lisa and Randy Herman

Illustration copyright 2010 Lisa and Randy Herman

1st printing, 2010
printed in China

ISBN-10: 0-9845532-0-7 (bound)

ISBN-13: 978-0-9845532-0-4 (bound)

Published in the United States by

Fredericka Books
2871 Wild Springs Lane
Corona, Ca 92883

For additional information about this book

please go to:

www. FREDDItheDOG.com

CPSIA Section 103(a) Compliant:
www.beaconstar.com/consumer
ID: K0114867
Tracking No.: K0212078-6816

Freddi the dog is the nicest,
sweetest, most lovable,
dog in the whole, entire world.

She doesn't have a mean bone
in her whole, entire body.

BUT!!!

She has one teeny, weeny, itsy, bitsy, tiny naughty bone!!!

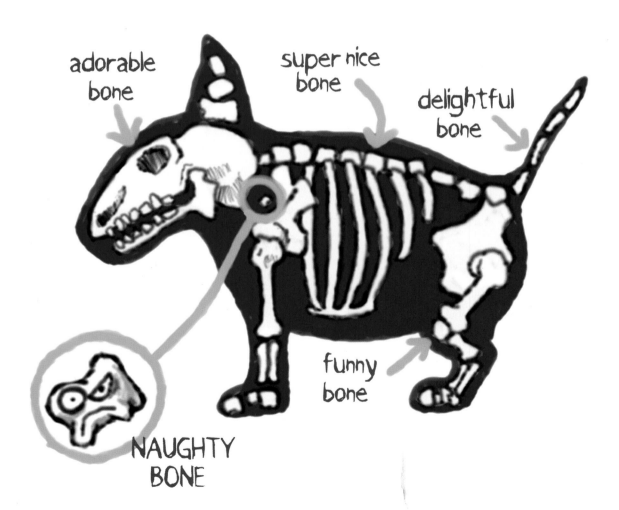

And if this naughty bone
gets tickled...

Freddi gets in...

One day Freddi's family went out.

And on that
day
Freddi's naughty bone
got
tickled.

And you know what happens when Freddi's naughty bone gets tickled?

Freddi gets in...

TROUBLE

Freddi started to
eat everything
in sight
And I mean
everything!!!

Freddi ate the telephone because it looked like a delicious hotdog.

Then she ate Aunt Martha's wig because she thought it was tasty spaghetti.

The next thing she ate was Grandpa Jo's underwear because it looked like smelly cheese.

Then she ate little Timmy's math homework because she thought it was toasted bread.

Freddi continued by eating Grandma Ruthy's hat because it looked like a cherry pie.

Then she ate a pillow because she thought it was a huge, giant marshmallow.

Sweet
Cherry Pie

Large
Marshmallow

Freddi chewed on the leather couch because she thought it was a huge chocolate bar.

Then she ate daddy's belt because it looked like chewy licorice.

Huge Chocolate Bar

Chewy Licorice

Freddi ate so much that day, that she got

soooo full.

The
whole house
was
a
BIG,
HUGE
mess.

So, when the family came

home that evening,

the father opened

the door and

yelled

Freddi was sent outside for a **"TIME OUT."**

But

Freddi got sick from all
the things she ate.
Freddi was

whining

and

moaning

all night long,

which woke up the family.

Mom and Dad realized

that Freddi was in a lot

of pain,

so they rushed her

to the vet

to see.....

Dr. Combover

Dr. Combover examined Freddi.
He poked and prodded,
but still couldn't understand why
Freddi was so sick.

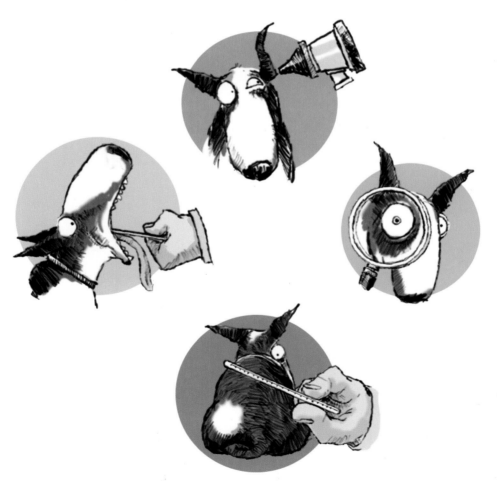

So, he ordered an X-ray for Freddi.

When Dr. Combover saw the x-ray, he couldn't believe his eyes.

There was a half-eaten telephone,
three quarters of a pillow,

a piece of a belt,

some stringy hair,

half a hat,

dirty, holey, underwear,

a whole math book with homework,

and a chunk of a brown leather sofa,

all stuffed in Freddi's belly.

"No wonder Freddi is not feeling well!!! She has half the house in her stomach!!"

Dr. Combover exclaimed in disbelief.

Freddi was rushed to the operating room.

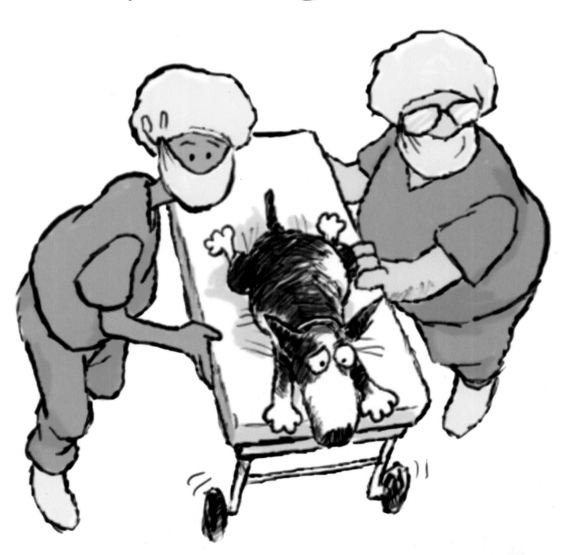

The family nervously waited in the waiting room.

Time was ticking by,
and still no word
from the doctor.

Suddenly they all heard a bark!!!

The **door** opened and Freddi
bolted **towards**
the family.

Everyone was **SO** happy
as Freddi licked their **faces.**

Freddi's family thanked
Dr. Combover,
and they took Freddi home
to get better.

Freddi learned her lesson,
not to eat or chew on
anything that does not belong
to her.

Perhaps now her eyes
will not be bigger
than her belly!!!